a cool moonlight

a cool moonlight

angela johnson

 DIAL BOOKS | NEW YORK

Published by Dial Books
A division of Penguin Group (USA) Inc.
345 Hudson Street
New York, New York 10014
Copyright © 2003 by Angela Johnson
Designed by Kimi Weart
Text set in Mrs. Eaves
Printed in the U.S.A. on acid-free paper
10 9 8 7 6 5 4 3 2 1

Library of Congress Cataloging-in-Publication Data

Johnson, Angela.
A cool moonlight / Angela Johnson.
p. cm.
Summary: Eight-year-old Lila, born with xeroderma pigmentosum,
a skin disease that makes her sensitive to sunlight, makes secret plans
to feel the sun's rays on her ninth birthday.
ISBN 0-8037-2846-8
[1. Skin—Diseases—Fiction. 2. Sisters—Fiction.
3. Imaginary friends—Fiction. 4. Sun—Fiction.] I. Title.
PZ7.J629 Co 2003
[Fic]—dc21
2002031521

For Jean Klasovsky
and a summer
of dreams

a cool moonlight

i don't remember the sun.

i don't remember the sun or how my sister, monk,
says it warms you up and feels good on your face
after dark sunless days in february. have there ever
been sunless days? i can't remember any of them.
do i just not remember or is my sister making up
stories like she always does?

i will ask elizabeth and alyssa. they will know.

elizabeth will probably just smile and whisper
softly.

alyssa will laugh loudly and jump around.

they know everything. secrets and light. light and secrets. they will know under the shadows of the vining moonflowers that we planted together in may. they will know as we move back and forth on the glider that sits in front of the fence that's protected by the old willow in our backyard.

they will know even though they say that they don't remember the sun either. i think that's just their way of being polite, like mama says people who come over for tea parties in my storybooks are.

elizabeth and alyssa will know because they are the best friends a girl who can't remember the sun or ever feel it on her face could have.

THE MOON

1

there are mushrooms that glow in the dark. did you know that? i have always known it, but i can't remember when or how i found out about them. i don't think i read it in a book. i only read books about witches and changelings and other stuff that i don't think is true, but might be.

i will ask elizabeth and alyssa when i found out about the glow-in-the-dark mushrooms. they'll know that too.

i'd ask my friend david, but he knows about

comic books more than anything else. i don't think he's ever mentioned mushrooms before.

elizabeth knows all the things that i need to know about the night. how to run in the night, find flowers in the night, and to listen in the night to everything that most people call quiet. it's real important to listen 'cause the night isn't quiet. it's the loudest real time in a twenty-four-hour day.

in the day there are no horns or people scream-ing or trucks' squealing brakes. all the real sounds get covered.

alyssa knows about people and the day. she likes people who laugh and shout and shine real bright. but she is nice about saying it's okay to live in the dark.

her voice is chirpy like a bird's when she talks. she puts her hands on her hips and nods her head fast.

so i believe her.

it's good to believe people.

i always do. i tell people all the time that i be-lieve them.

alyssa says it's because i'm not nine yet like her.

when i'm nine, i'll know better than to believe folks. i think how sad it's going to be in two months that i won't believe anybody anymore.

but the two months will give me time. it will give me time to do what i've been planning for so long. elizabeth and alyssa will keep the secret 'cause too many people shouldn't know. it's better that way.

so i sit and wait for them against the fence gate. if it's like all the nights before this one, alyssa will come under the fence first, then elizabeth.

sometimes elizabeth will be in a tutu and sun hat and her yellow rain boots, smiling and quiet.

alyssa will be in a cape covering a long cotton slip that's too big for her and new white canvas tennis shoes, jumping and laughing.

she always wears the shoes and they're always white. and even though i have my dark sunglasses on in the night, her shoes always glow like the mushrooms. they almost look alive, like they could walk right off her feet and run around the backyard all by themselves.

* ★ *

i have to cover up. clothes, clothes, clothes.

the night is good to me. the sunlight hurts. it has since the day i was born. even some light that isn't the real sun can hurt me, like the light from a juke-box. i just cover up all the time. mama feels better if i do.

it's 'cause of my chromosomes. they can't protect me from the sun. i could be burnt and even go blind if the sun gets to me.

all our windows keep the sun out, though.

my sister, monk, says we are shadow people and proud of it.

the rule is only wait a while. but a while doesn't have a real time limit like five minutes or eight minutes, so a while is as long as i feel like waiting, i guess.

once, a while was almost when the sun was com-ing up. elizabeth and alyssa shimmied under the fence, and when they got close, i saw their faces were covered with chocolate and cookie crumbs. alyssa's cape was torn and she started telling me a story about bank robbers who would give them a million dollars if they climbed a mountain for it.

elizabeth giggled and said it was true. she'd lost her sun hat when they met bigfoot near the top of the mountain.

a few minutes later, though, mama came out and said that the light was coming and it was time for me to go in.

mama stood looking at us with her hands on her hips for a long time. she kept on looking at elizabeth and alyssa way after i went through the kitchen door. she stared at them out the uv-blocking tinted windows of the kitchen.

then mama did something that made me jump. she went over, real close to alyssa, and looked at her. i thought alyssa would run away, but she stood there like she didn't even see mama. smiling.

elizabeth crossed her arms real tight and backed against the fence.

i guess some mountain-climbing girls are careful.

the last i saw of them for a couple of nights was alyssa's white tennis shoes disappearing under the fence. but in the coming morning light, they'd lost their glow.

2

i like the grocery store at night.

i push the cart down the aisles while dad stares at the backs of boxes and cans. he doesn't hold the frozen food like he does the warm food. too cold, i guess, so he just throws it in the moving cart.

he has to be fast 'cause i am.

i am the best grocery cart racer there ever was. at least i'm the best in the store right now. i rest when i get to the end of the aisles, but take the turns so fast i'm almost invisible.

dad is calling me. "lila?"

i holler to him from two rows away. "what do you want? i'm racing."

"lila?"

it's funny, us calling to each other from a long way away. dad's voice is real loud and echoes in the store.

"what?" i say again, and start putting three packages of cookies underneath the broccoli, bananas, and onions. sometimes dad doesn't know that he wants good things like cookies and candy. sometimes i just have to help him out.

now he's walking toward me with his own cart.

"baby, i need you not to scream in the store."

"but you were screaming to *me,* dad."

he looks at me, smiles, and shakes his head at the cart. first i think he's noticed all the chocolate cookies i hid, but he hasn't. he looks down at my cart and kicks one of the wheels.

"pretty good tires, kid. she looks like a good racer. you run her much?"

my dad is tall and skinny and always wears striped shirts. his eyes are brown and he has a bald head. i watch him shave it sometimes. it makes me laugh. it used to make monk laugh too, but she doesn't watch him anymore.

i guess she thinks it's babyish to watch dad shave now.

but that's okay. i watch her too. i watch the way she puckers her lips when she starts to put on lipstick. i watch the way she sprays perfume on herself before she goes out for the night.

sometimes she's better than the movies.

and sometimes watching my mama is even better than watching dad or monk. mama takes longer. she says it's because she wants to look like she's not wearing any makeup at all.

i don't understand that.

but i guess i don't understand a lot.

a minute later dad and me are in a race. we roll down the frozen food aisle, around the vegetable bins, then knock over toilet paper and napkins when we wreck in the paper lane.

dad isn't as good as me 'cause he's too tall. he can't bend down and move like he's part of the metal cart. he's not bad, though, and almost beats me to the soap aisle.

i like shopping at night. nobody but us and a lady in a nurse's uniform are in the aisles right now. it's two in the morning and dad doesn't go to work until four-thirty in the day.

he says he's kind of like me. he sleeps in the morning and hardly sees the sun. i don't think he misses the daylight that much, though, 'cause besides me he's the best middle-of-the-night grocery cart racer there ever was.

when we get up to the counter, the nurse is in front of us. she smells like peppermint. i wonder if she works with my eye doctor. his office always smells like peppermint.

dad rolls out our groceries into the parking lot and loads them into the trunk. then he picks me up and puts me in the cart. we race around and around the empty parking lot, with me looking up to the sky so i won't get dizzy.

we drive home and i must fall asleep, 'cause when i wake, dad is carrying me in his arms across the yard, toward our house under a cool moonlight.

3

the first time me and monk baked cookies i drank almost half a bottle of vanilla before i figured out it didn't taste like i thought it would. got sick right there on the kitchen counter. how could vanilla not taste as good as it smells?

the sweet smell curls up all in the corners of the house, then draws you down to the kitchen. but it lies, vanilla.

i asked monk if we could bake the cookies without it.

"no, we can't. the cookies would taste nasty."

that was monk's favorite word then. *nasty*.

rainy days were nasty. her best friend's brother's car was nasty, and anything that didn't make her happy the very minute she thought about it was nasty.

i smiled at monk. i thought then that i liked her better than anybody in the whole world.

she always picked me over her friends, and i know that most older sisters wouldn't do that.

she's had some practice watching over me.

she was the one who used to come to my class from her high school around the corner every two hours when i was in first grade and put more sunblock on me. every two hours no matter what, they would let her out of class to do that for me. she says that's how she remembers tenth grade: her hands smelling of sunblock.

i wouldn't let my teacher do it at first. i didn't know her hands. monk's hands were soft and knowing. they never missed a spot.

she turned the cookie dough with the same know-ing hands.

"more oatmeal or more chocolate chips, lila?" she asked that time.

"neither. raisins," i said.

monk turned up her nose. "i hate raisins. pick something else."

"it can only be raisins, monk. just raisins."

"why only raisins? we could even put in apricots, nuts . . ."

i put my hand into the bowl with monk's. the cookie dough was warm and my fingers went right through the oatmeal. too smooth.

"no. only raisins."

then i pointed at the box. "see, monk, it says they've been kissed by the sun. i want all things that have been kissed by the sun."

monk poured raisins into the dough until i told her to stop. we plop-plopped them down onto the cookie sheet. the raisins stuck out everywhere.

monk let me slide the pan into the warm oven.

i couldn't wait for the smell. and the kissed-by-the-sun part too.

i remember wondering if the cookies would glow and make shadows when the raisins had melted and spread a little. i kind of knew they wouldn't, but i had to ask monk.

"will they, monk?"

monk was putting the butter away and singing.

"will they what, lila?"

"will the cookies glow like the sun? make shadows and warm things up 'cause they've been kissed by the sun?"

"maybe."

"really?" i said, and got even more excited.

i couldn't sit still waiting for them to come out of the oven. the cookies glowing would make up for me not being allowed to be kissed by the sun.

monk swept the kitchen floor. flour was everywhere.

"go upstairs and put on more sunblock," she said. "don't miss a spot."

she should have known i never did. i still don't. my hands are smaller than hers, but i think they know just as much.

the cookies didn't smell as good leaving the kitchen as they did going back, so i jumped the last three steps to get back faster.

and it was all better than vanilla could ever have been.

better than when ice cream runs down your arms and you catch it while it's still cold.

better than when monk plays her violin and mama cries.

the cookies were glowing. still on the baking sheet, right there on the counter. glowing. they'd been kissed by the sun so much that the light ran right off the cookies and onto the pan.

i sat in the moon-shadowy kitchen at the counter and smiled at the cookies and then at monk for whatever magic she had that made me even forgive vanilla. and that let me know that the sun—if it wants—might run out of the cookies, all around the

house, then out into the world with me having
finally seen it.

no matter what i bake now, there are raisins,
always raisins.

4

i feel like i've been eight for practically a hundred years. i wonder if i'm the oldest eight-year-old in the world. if i stay eight any longer, i will have gray hair when i turn nine, like the lady at the news-paper stand who always smiles at me when monk takes me there.

i feel what mama calls blue. it's been a while since i've seen alyssa and elizabeth. i wonder if they think about me and the back garden when they aren't around.

i've been thinking about them when i go to sleep, right before the sun rises, and just before i wake up, around lunchtime.

monk must know something is wrong 'cause at dinner she gives me her fish sticks. mama and dad raise their eyebrows but keep talking about how things are slow down at the music store.

then monk says, "want to go for a ride tonight, lila?"

i do, and nod my head 'cause my mouth is full of fish sticks.

i like driving around with monk at night. her old car is like her bedroom. lots of stuff on the floor and always something good to eat in the glove compart- ment or under the seat. it can be like a library too.

in between here and there is the perfect time to read.

monk has nighttime free for me 'cause she goes to college in the day and lives at home with us. she says it's not time for her to leave yet.

i'm glad.

*   ★   *

i was born when monk was nine. almost like me now.

two days after i was born, mama put me out in the backyard in the shade so i could get some air. by the time she looked over at me again, the august sun had crept up and burnt my leg.

mama says i screamed real bad.

and because a pediatrician at the hospital had seen xeroderma pigmentosum when he was in medical school, he had the test run on me. then everybody found out i had a defect that made me sensitive to the light. the sun. uv rays. some street-lights.

the first time anybody was ever mean to me about my xp was mitchell forte in kindergarten. he called me vampire girl and got yelled at so bad by his mom i almost felt bad for him. almost.

never mind.

i'm going driving with monk. when she was my age, she already knew how to wrap me up and

sunblock me. and sometimes i wonder if at eight-
een she feels older than everybody.

monk's car is like a lazy old dog that moves only if
you pat its head and feed it franks from the refrig-
erator. monk calls her minnie bell and is always
talking real sweet and low to her when it's time to
start the ignition.

  i walk out of the house with my hood up, sunscreen
underneath my long-sleeve shirt and khakis. i watch
the streetlights glow green behind my sunglasses.

  monk is humming behind the wheel before i get
in the car.

  "will she start or won't she?" monk says.

  i smile at the little rusty white bug 'cause she really
does look like a spotted puppy. i pat her above the
headlight eyes.

  as we back out of the driveway, minnie bell's head-
lights shine into the backyard and i think i catch a
reflection of alyssa's shoes. i hope they'll stay until
i get back.

monk's car bumps out of the drive and she says maybe the transmission is going.

"what's the transmission do?" i say.

"it's important to the car, lila."

i guess a lot of things might be important to the car. like the glove compartment. it must really be important. monk keeps extra sunglasses and sunblock in there for me. i keep candy bars and other stuff i might need on the nights that monk takes me for drives around the city.

it's my best time. it's the time that ticks in my heart a day before we do it. tick, tick, tick.

soon we are leaving our neighborhood. gone into the night, and off to the city to see monk's college friends. soon i won't feel eight and old. soon i'll just feel the night.

5

after we go over the bridge, minnie bell starts to purr as we drive into the city. she's warm now. monk races taxis and usually wins. you wouldn't even know minnie bell in the city. it seems to be only a few minutes before we're parked one block from the cafe.

a man waiting to cross the street with us looks down and says to me, "you cold, little chicky? you got enough clothes on, huh?"

monk looks at him and laughs. then i look at her

and do the same thing.

he shrugs his shoulders and runs across the street when the light changes.

when he's almost half a block ahead of us, he yells, "it's your world, little chicky." then he waves and runs down the subway stairs.

monk hugs me and whispers in my ear, "it sure is, chicky, it sure is."

pavel, noah, and detra sip coffee at the fallen angel beanery across the street from my favorite deli in the city. when they see monk coming through the door (i see them before they see us), they yell both our names out and wave us over to their booth.

soon monk is drinking coffee and having the waitress bring me raisin muffins. i listen to them and slurp my smoothie. i always do. i like to go back to what i know.

detra gets up and goes over to the jukebox and puts in about a hundred quarters. it's all for me. she plays every single song i like on the jukebox.

all for me.

then i start wandering around the fallen angel, looking and listening. i want to go over to the juke-box to watch the records change, but i can't get that close to the light off the box. the rest of the light in the angel is okay, though.

there is a chair that rocks (it's not supposed to) over by the big windows and a purple couch with yellow polka dots that's squishy to sit on and swallows you up.

the angel has mr. rocko too, a mannequin who monk says was rescued from the fashion district by one of the waitresses. and because she hasn't told me which waitress, i figure it's the one with the really big afro and the tattoo of the dragonfly on her ankle.

it makes me smile to think of her and mr. rocko running down the street, her saving him from a life in a store window. the dragonfly waitress must be the angel that the coffeehouse is named after.

mr. rocko could dress a little better, considering he was saved by an angel. he needs to wear something besides that old fireman's hat and apron i see him in all the time. he got santa boots last year, but he still needs more clothes. his angel should have got him some from where he used to live before she brought him here.

but that's okay.

'cause soon i'm dancing to a song that talks about the moonlight being a fine and natural sight. i don't even notice mr. rocko anymore. i'm thinking about how my feet spin over the wooden floor and it doesn't even squeak.

i catch sight of pavel smiling at me from the table and pointing at another smoothie for me. but i dance on.

i know what it's like to dance in the moonlight, so i don't even have to close my eyes that much to be in the dark woods or anywhere that the moonlight is streaming through. but that doesn't make me stop wondering, 'cause i always do. i'm wondering what it must feel like to dance in the sunlight.

and maybe i wouldn't even dance. maybe i'd just

wear a slip like alyssa in the sunlight and run through other people's yards.

maybe that's all i'd do. maybe.

but then i remember i haven't ever seen alyssa and elizabeth in the daylight either. they always leave to go back home when the sun is coming up.

i sit back down, thinking about the girls, drinking my smoothies and listening to monk and her friends laugh and talk about college and jobs till my head slumps over on detra.

the last thing i remember is mr. rocko smiling at me from across the road.

when me and monk are heading back over the bridge, i burp strawberries and listen to her talk about how one day she wants to learn to swim without grabbing hold of the person next to her when a wave hits her.

"just swim in pools, monk," i say.

she looks at me like she never thought of that before.

"good idea, little chicky."

i press my face against the window as we leave the city behind. we drive into the dark, the moon sometimes our only light besides streetlamps. i feel warm and sleepy going away from the city lights.

6

dad just finished my clubhouse out of the
leftover wood and other stuff he used when he made
the bathroom bigger.

lila is written on a piece of wood right over the
door. i added stars and butterflies all over it in yellow and purple.

monk asks, "don't you want to put a *keep out* sign
over the door?"

i don't.

then she says, "it's not a clubhouse unless you

don't want some people in the club."

"why would i want to keep people out?" i say.

monk says, "i don't know. people always do. it's stupid, but there it is."

"if you think it's stupid, monk, why do you want me to do it?"

i poke my head into the cool dark of the club. it doesn't feel real yet 'cause nobody has been in it except me when dad was measuring to see if i'd have headroom. the clubhouse even has a skylight made of plexiglas.

i say, "i like company, monk. i can't wait till alyssa and elizabeth see this. they can be the first members."

monk smiles that smile she does when i talk about my friends, then scratches the back of her arm and yawns. she almost says something, then decides not to. she always does that—changes her mind at the start of a sentence. i can't do that. i can't stop what is coming out of my mouth.

monk knows how to save her words.

she'd have a million dollars if her saved words counted as money. maybe more.

"do what you want with your clubhouse. what do you need to make it comfortable?"

we spend the next couple of hours dragging out big floor pillows, posters, cups, a pink flamingo from the basement, and a plastic bag full of cookies.

now all i have to do is wait.

monk goes into the house and hollers to anybody who can hear her that she's going to study for a test she has tomorrow and doesn't want anybody to bother her.

i walk around my clubhouse, touching all the sharp edges and places that i think might look better with yellow paint that glows in the dark.

is there such a paint?

i'll ask later, but now i wait.

"where you been?" i ask alyssa. she never answers, but i think it's polite to ask about other people. like you care about them.

alyssa's cape drags the ground, but i don't notice it as much as i notice the new fairy wings on the back of it.

alyssa points and says, "where i always am," which is someplace past our back fence and across the field behind it. i've never been to their house, so i just nod.

elizabeth comes out from behind her and screams, "yahh!"

she has fairy wings on too. they are baby pink with pearls around the edges. alyssa's are white with pink glitter through and through. and because they know i am watching them, they grab hands and dance around the yard with their backs to me to show off their wings.

they are magic in tutus, capes, and wings, and it seems to me they almost float to the roof of my club-house. because it's dark, they run into each other and fall down laughing. i want to be like them.

lighter than air.

i want to wear only a slip and white tennis shoes

that glow in the dark and are not for protection.

i want a sun hat like elizabeth's that is a sun hat 'cause that's what it lets in with the big holes all over it.

we are planning for just that time. they're the only ones who know i'm going to leave the moonlight castle. i'm going to dance in the light of my backyard real soon. we've been talking about it for a long time. they say they'll dance with me.

i run to them as they're climbing to the top of the clubhouse. when i am standing by the door, they look at each other, then me, and flap their arms like they are going to fly right off the house.

fly into the night.

fly into the stars.

but instead they grab my hands and pull me up on top of the clubhouse with them. i don't remember when it was that elizabeth took off her wings and put them on me. it's not important, i guess, 'cause now i have wings. and elizabeth whispers in my ear that they are mine.

we might as well be on the roof of the tallest building in the world as we flap our arms and call out into the night.

one day we'll be calling out to the sun.

THE STARS

7

some days things are blurry coming from my eyes. when i tell mama this, she looks worried and says it's time for an eye doctor visit.

blurry eyes with xp is not a good thing.

sometimes i think i see stars.

we go to dr. morton because he sees patients at night.

it's funny when dr. morton looks into my eyes and makes faces. the light he shines from the little stick sometimes makes me want to giggle. i try not to, though.

"please don't blink," the doctor says.

i giggle anyway and think about the smell in the room. peppermint.

"why peppermint?"

"what, lila? did you say something?"

i must have whispered it.

i said, "why does your office smell like peppermint?"

dr. morton smiles at me, then at my mama.

"i didn't know it did."

"yeah, you know—like the bottom of people's grandma's purses."

dr. morton laughs and says, "my grandmother's purse always smelled like licorice."

then he laughs some more, like he's going to tell me a story. i like his stories. they always start off with him saying, "now, you won't believe this."

but i always do.

i like it when he laughs. his big face wrinkles and

his eyes light up like fireflies in the backyard. he laughs so much i don't even get scared anymore when i see his white coat that matches his teeth and hair.

it used to make me cry when i'd see a white coat.

that meant crying when i'd see the people at the deli counter at russo's and even a chef in a restaurant who might come out and speak to people.

mama says she's glad that's all over with.

i do like dr. morton, though. he makes sure people's eyes work right and tells them what to do if they don't.

and his office smells like gum.

dr. morton sends me out of the room and talks to mama. when they come out of the office, he's carrying big wraparound sunglasses.

"you should wear these when you're awake," he says.

i take them from him, then look up at mama's sad face and put them on.

8

alyssa and elizabeth climb in my window
from the tree outside. the leaves bounce up and
down.

i'm so happy to see them.

elizabeth waves, opens up a book, sits under the
window, and reads about unicorns.

this is the first time i've seen them in the early
morning with the sun all the way up. but i'm safe in
my room with my dark windows and blinds.

The girls don't glow and sparkle in the day, but

that's okay. i think maybe the daylight takes away
some of the glow—you know, like how you have to
put those stick-on ceiling stars in your hand, cover
them up, and squint to see them in the day.

i wonder if the girls even know they glow in the
dark.

alyssa crawls across the floor and up onto my bed.
she slips under my spaceship blanket and moves next
to me. there's a crumpled bag in her hand.

"here," she says, and smiles.

"thanks. do you like my room?"

alyssa moves from underneath the spaceships and
starts touching everything. i notice when she's
crawling on the floor and picking up toys (which i
was supposed to pick up last night) that she's not
wearing wings. she's just got on a long t-shirt that
says *bob's diner*.

and i wonder, as she talks to my stuffed bunny
with one ear, who bob is.

maybe i'll ask her later.

"what's her name?" she says, squeezing the bunny.

"she's just bunny."

alyssa moves around the room with bunny in her hand. she touches the walls, she touches the books on my desk that me and monk just painted sky blue. she touches my fuzzy slippers that stick out of my closet.

"yes, i like your room, lila. can i have it?"

elizabeth giggles.

i jump off my bed and cross the room to sit by my closet. it's my second favorite place to sit (the kitchen is my favorite), 'cause you can watch the sun rise through the tree outside my window. then i start laughing when alyssa finds more things that she needs to have.

"you can have what you want because this is the first time you've been in my room."

alyssa drops the yo-yo, umbrella, cowgirl hat, and the bag of pretty marbles that she'd put in her t-shirt pocket. she keeps bunny, though, smiles, and sits down right by me, then points to the bag on the bed.

"it's in there. it's the first thing."

i look at the old wrinkled market bag and think how it just doesn't look like anything good could be in it. but you never can tell.

she says, "you know about where the other things will come from, don't you?"

i nod and remember the rainy night we talked about how everything would happen. alyssa and elizabeth would fill the bag. we just wouldn't know when they'd find things for it.

surprises all around.

alyssa puts her hands on my face.

"i had to fight a bear to get it."

"a real bear?" i say, and think that there's not a better friend in the world than alyssa even though i know there aren't any bears in the neighborhood.

alyssa laughs so hard, she falls against me, and elizabeth stops reading for a minute and laughs too.

then i start laughing.

when i stop, i say, "i hope you remember it's got to be a secret."

"it is," alyssa says.

"nobody can know except me, you, and elizabeth."

"uh-huh, lila."

"elizabeth knows it's a secret too, right?"

alyssa is on her back blowing spit bubbles now.

"elizabeth won't tell. she knows all about secrets and paper bags."

elizabeth nods to her book.

"okay," i say, and think about blowing spit bubbles too.

"anyway, lila, who would we tell about the sun bag?"

and now i start to wonder just who they would tell. nobody, i guess. just nobody.

and it will be a surprise this way. it will be a surprise real soon when everybody sees me walking, running, and turning cartwheels in the sun. so i guess they don't have to know about the sun bag magic yet.

they don't have to know.

a few minutes later the girls climb back out the window into the sun and are gone before i can tell alyssa that bunny has fallen out of her pocket.

i lay bunny on my desk for alyssa next time, then put the sun bag under my bed and think about breakfast and secrets.

9

when i was real little, i used to think that one day i'd get a big old jar full of fireflies and set them on top of our house. and when i'd go out at night to play in the yard, they'd light up like the sun.

doesn't really work like that, i guess, and i don't want to put fireflies in jars anyway. the thought of sun on top of the house at night shining down on our yard is a good one, though.

* ★ *

i crawl under my bed and pull the sun bag from underneath it. the bag looks about a hundred years old and has pictures of dinosaurs and trees drawn all over it. elizabeth must have drawn them.

she always talks about dinosaurs. they ate trees. she even says she sees them on street corners and near the park. but because there's no way it's true, it's just fun to listen to her stories.

i open the bag and the thing in it shines so brightly, i have to close it real fast. i hug it close to me. it feels warm.

after a while i just count the dinosaurs and trees on the bag. i notice that some of the dinosaurs have wings and that other ones are wearing tutus and rain boots.

it makes me laugh so hard, mama knocks on my door.

"what's up, kid?"

"just laughing."

mama leans against the door and looks around my room. i guess she doesn't see anything funny, but she smiles anyway. then she leans over and picks bunny off my dresser.

"i haven't seen bunny in a long time," she says.

"that's okay, mama—she hasn't seen you in a long time either."

"do you want me to fix her ear, lila?"

"no. she belongs to alyssa now and she doesn't mind that bunny has only one ear. i don't think it makes any difference to a rabbit's hearing if it has only one ear. the other one's big enough to hear everything."

"okay. no fixing bunny's ear."

mama slides her feet in and out of her clogs that she's glued diamonds and rubies on. not real ones, but still shiny and big. she loves gluing stuff.

i lean over and put my hands on her shoes. she can't really go anyplace now. but instead of staying, she steps out of her clogs, leans down, and puts them on my feet.

"i have to go to the mall. you gonna be okay here for a minute?"

"uh-huh."

"okay. i'm gone. see you later."

"see you later."

for the rest of the morning i clump around upstairs in mama's clogs. clump, clump. and when i remember that dad is sleeping i take them off and put them on the dresser where bunny used to live.

i put bunny over by the window for alyssa, then go downstairs to get a snack. when i get back to my room, i open the bag and there's even more light coming out than before.

10

david gallucci and me once got locked in his garage for most of the night. we ate twenty-three popsicles out of their deepfreeze before his dad found us. their garage isn't connected to their house. i guess they made it soundproof or something.

i ate all the grape popsicles and david ate the rest.

his brother ben closed us in with the garage door opener, then he went to a basketball game. we were stuck in the garage long enough for our parents to look all over the place for us. we couldn't hear them calling, though.

so we had to eat all the popsicles.

david and me have been friendly since way before elizabeth and alyssa and me.

we used to eat mud together and dress david's sister's cat in my doll clothes. the cat still doesn't like us much even though we don't do that anymore.

david leaves his house early in the morning, walks down the sidewalk, turns right, and crosses the street a minute later to go to school. but we're still friends.

my school is in the living room and sometimes in the kitchen when mama's cooking.

today i learned how to say *dog* and *cat* in five languages, and when david walks through the kitchen door, i'm just finishing a diorama of a native american village from the 1700s.

he waves to mama, who's cleaning something green out of the fridge, walks over to me, and bites into an apple he takes out of his backpack.

"cool," he says when he sees the diorama.

"yeah," i say.

there's glue, paper, toothpicks, and other stuff that me and mama found in drawers all over the kitchen. i like the kitchen when it's a mess. it feels warm and good.

we both look at the village until i almost feel like i'm in it. i even think i smell the smoke from the fire that i made out of foil and painted with red nail polish. i like the way it shines.

it's a nighttime village. there's a moon painted in the back and bats flying around. everybody is sitting around the fire and telling stories. at least i think that's what they're doing.

david says, "they're talking about the hunt they had today. the warrior hunters are telling a story about how the buffalo were brave, but they were braver. they tell how they rode their horses into the setting sun when it was all over."

"was the sun beautiful, david?" i whisper.

david moves in closer to the village. he pulls up a

stool and sits at the counter so he can see better.

"it was so beautiful, they made up a song for how beautiful it was."

"did they dance to the song?"

"the whole village danced."

"was it a long dance?"

david bites his apple and thinks.

"the dance was so long, it took seven days and seven nights to finish. it started with the kids. the chief's children were the first to start dancing around the night fire, which is pretty cool when you think how our parents won't even let us stand near a warm stove."

"yeah," i say, looking across the kitchen at mama.

"then the other children started one by one . . ."

i stare at the village and the action-figure people i dressed in clothes i made from looking at a history book.

guess i did a good job.

"did they all dance together in the end?"

"yeah, but it took days to finish. other villages

heard the song and came to dance. the music spread and the dance was bigger than any of the people had ever seen."

"were all the villages friends with the others after the dance?"

david thinks for a minute.

"no, they weren't friends. but they weren't the enemies they used to be. they understood better now."

"understood what?" i ask.

"that you don't always have to understand people's ways to get along with them."

i like that they understood better.

sometimes all i want is for people not to stare at me. for people to understand.

i like my village better than i ever thought i could now that david has told me about it. even though david is a day person and walks away to school with everybody else, he's special.

he sees things and knows stuff.

i can see his red curls underneath his baseball

cap. they match his freckles. once we tried to count them, but gave up after the first hundred. i think he gets more as he gets older.

i'll tell david about the sun bag. he should know about it 'cause he knows how important the sun is. i can tell from his story about the villagers who danced.

i know i should tell him about the bag by the way he looked at my village under the moon.

11

minnie bell is sick and has to be pulled by a big tow truck out of our driveway. monk looks sad. she shakes her head and goes back into the house.

the fireflies are out and so is david.

this is the night when i want him to meet elizabeth and alyssa 'cause he never has before. he always just misses them when his mom calls him in from next door. screams, really. i think she thinks david has bad hearing.

she says she screams so she doesn't have to call him a second time.

david is on his bike tearing through the front yards of all the neighbors. he's chasing fireflies. i skate along the sidewalks on my rollerblades as all the streetlights pop on.

i can stand under these lights. they don't have the rays that can hurt like some of the older street-lights.

one.

two.

three.

four.

all the way down the street we follow the lights as they turn on in a line.

"can you hear it, david?"

"not yet."

"can you see it?"

"no."

at the end of our street is the house that lights

up just as all the streetlights pop on. monk says the lights are on timers to keep burglars away.

you hear it first, but you have to stand in the yard overgrown by azaleas. you can barely see the house for the azalea bushes.

first there's a hum, then a flash, then a song. the old dark house nobody ever comes out of in the daytime lights up the whole street and plays music. you can count on your fingers when it's going to happen.

i whisper, "one, two, three. light."

and then i think i see a bird flying in the window. but do birds hum like the house does? this bird's wings are real big.

and do birds laugh?

one, two, three. light.

david starts riding his bike across the yards again. he could get away with it in the dark if he wanted to, but usually he yells after he flies out of each yard.

"c'mon, lila. let's go."

i start skating back over the smooth sidewalks to

my house. out of the corner of my eye i see somebody looking out of the dark house.

but whoever owns the house doesn't live there.
monk says so.

my skates make a whizzing noise along the way
back home. when i get there, all the streetlights are
on and david is waiting for me in our driveway.

the driveway looks empty without minnie bell.
mama's car can't make up for her being gone. i try
not to think about her in an old scary car-fix place
as i head back to my clubhouse with david to wait for
alyssa and elizabeth.

"what do they look like, lila? are they our age? do
they live in this neighborhood? are they home-
schooled like you or do they go to some other
school?"

david leans back against the clubhouse and looks
up at the stars.

he has waited for them with me before.

he's tried a lot of times, but they never show up

when he's here. then his mom calls him, he leaves, and they come. it has always been like that.

"maybe it's not meant to be," dad said once about all my friends meeting each other. "the girls are pretty shy. i've never even seen them."

"mama has," i said.

dad nodded and kept on reading the newspaper. he's never home when the girls come out. he works late at the music store in the night and was asleep the time they visited me in the day.

i should have woken him up.

but now me and david wait.

david takes a bag of dried apples out of his pocket and passes them to me. they're good and chewy while we both look up at the stars and talk about nothing.

david's mom calls him and i think maybe he should pretend he doesn't hear her. we could just say nothing and sit in the clubhouse waiting for elizabeth and alyssa forever.

"sorry, lila."

"you gonna go, then? maybe if you waited . . ."

david looks at the fence next door. "she doesn't like to call me twice."

"okay. i'll tell them you were here."

david gives me the rest of the dried apples and gets ready to go, but turns back around. i can see his face shining in the moonlight.

"tell 'em i'll see them soon. tell 'em i'll see them."

"i will."

"tell 'em i can help them with the sun bag stuff."

"i will."

david slips out of the clubhouse, asks me to look after his bike, then goes over the fence instead of underneath it like alyssa and elizabeth do.

in a second he's gone.

then i see white tennis shoes coming under the fence, then a silver tutu and alyssa. and in another second there's a pink tutu and elizabeth.

then there's the stars and us and the moon.

12

david drops by on his way to school.

he says he had butterfly dreams last night.

it's weird 'cause he usually has only superhero dreams or dreams about monsters that knock over his house and crush his school into a million pieces.

he likes those dreams.

he says he usually wakes up from them wanting to eat a whole lot of breakfast. but the butterfly dream made him think about flying and not in a cape as a mutant, so he didn't like it much.

he says that the butterflies were really girls who laughed at him a lot and carried paper bags in their hands. so i figure he must have been having a dream about alyssa and elizabeth.

then he pulls a paper bag out from behind his back.

the bag makes me smile. there's a message on the side of it that is surrounded by dinosaurs. it says, *always ready to be filled*.

when david leaves, i open the bag 'cause i want to see.

and it shines so bright when i open it, just like david said it did for him, that i smile even more as i eat my cereal.

dad comes in through the back door.

"what's up, kid?"

dad's face has crinkles around his eyes and he looks a little tired. after the music store closes, he stays there and works on all the paper. at least that's what mama says he does.

but i think he plays cds and dances around the store. or he plays some of the videos and puts his feet up to watch them. i would if you left me in the store all night long.

"nothing's up but the sun, moon, and stars, a few birds, some planes . . ."

"okay, okay," he says, then moves over to the coffeemaker and pours a big cup into his moose mug. "where's mama?"

"she took monk to school. minnie bell got sick after you left yesterday."

"too bad. but she's old. it happens. what you going to learn today, chicky?" (dad likes my new nickname.)

i hold on tight to the bag alyssa and elizabeth left with david to give to me and only just now know why they did it. they could have given it to me last night.

i jump off the stool, hug dad, then run out of the kitchen up the stairs and put the bag with the other one.

i meet dad on the way back down. he's heading
up to bed.

"i'm going to learn to wait for stuff to happen
and still be surprised when it does," i say.

THE SUN

13

you can see the city lights past the trees at night
in my neighborhood. the city glows over the hous-
es and trees.

it glows past the grocery stores and wendy's water
park at the edge of town. it glows past everything i
know. and in the night with the city glowing behind
us i go with monk to all the big mike department
stores.

monk is a secret shopper.

it sounds like spy stuff, secret shopping. i wondered if she got to wear dark glasses and a cape to all the stores, but she told me it wasn't like that.

all she does is go in shops, banks, or wherever her job tells her to go and ask questions about different things, then writes everything down afterward and gives it to her boss.

monk says i make her seem like a real shopper. you know, a little sister who's always asking for something or jumping up and down by the check-out place for candy bars or the plastic toys they sell there.

tonight monk and me go to three big mike stores. i'm wearing my red riding hood cape. it's my favorite, and when i wear it, monk calls me hood. i like that, even though monk says a hood isn't always a good thing.

we must seem real to the store lady when i keep pulling monk's arm to go or to buy me some sparkly tennis shoes. finally the store lady gives me some gum.

monk winks at me when the lady isn't looking at

us anymore 'cause she's finding out if any of their stores carry a special kind of lotion. the lady is nice and even smiles when she makes the phone calls to the other stores.

i get bored and start skipping through the aisles. and that's when i see them. alyssa and elizabeth. but at first i don't know it's them 'cause sometimes big mike's is full of people at night and you can't tell who they are when they're all squished up together.

but it's them.

no wings.

no tutus or rain boots.

just plain old sweatshirts and jeans. they're holding each other's hands and moving real slow behind a lady on crutches pushing a cart.

i move closer to them. the lady on crutches is wearing sunglasses just like me.

i feel sorry for the lady. the cast must itch her 'cause she's scratching underneath it with a long stick.

i run at them, thinking they'll see me and dance

around or want to play. but it doesn't happen that way.

"hey alyssa, elizabeth."

they move closer to each other and smile at me, but i turn away to call monk, and when i look back, they're gone.

i was about to say to them, "i've never seen you two in the store. i'm here with monk, but it's a secret. minnie bell is fixed now and we drove her here. where are your tutus and did you like david?"

but they're gone and the lady is looking at me funny. she walks away shaking her head.

maybe she doesn't like my red riding hood cape or the way i wear dark glasses like her.

monk finds me a few minutes later and says that she's finished and that this big mike's is the best she's gone to so far. i wrap my arms around her and say i'm tired and want to go home. so we do.

14

)

david comes over after school and we lie on the living room floor and read nine years' worth of my favorite comic book, the magnificent mutants. talia tears is my favorite mutant. she's water.

she can swim forever in the ocean and never have to come up for air. she can go under doors and people just think that their water pipes broke. pretty cool. and i like the boots she wears. they look like fins.

david likes luke dracon. he can breathe fire and fly all over the world without ever resting.

but even though talia and luke are mutant friends, they are the worst people for each other. heat makes talia boil (like me) and she loses her power. water puts out luke's fire. but i guess it's okay now 'cause in most of the comics i read about them, they look like they worked all that stuff out. "like friends do," david says.

the friend thing's not always easy.

i tell david about seeing alyssa and elizabeth in big mike's the other night.

"are you sure it was them?"

"yep."

david rolls up the comic book he's reading. "it could have been two kids who looked just like them. you told me they never leave the neighborhood."

"no," i say, knowing it had to be them. "i told you i'd never *seen* them out of the neighborhood. it was them, though. and the lady on crutches must have been their mom."

"maybe," david says.

"you think she's somebody else."

"don't know."

"who could the lady be if she's not their mom?"

i couldn't tell if alyssa and elizabeth even looked like the crutch lady 'cause she had on dark glasses. it bothered me.

david puts his magnificent mutants down.

"do you have any more of those marshmallow cookies?"

"yep," i say, then keep on reading about how talia tears went on vacation to the desert. she didn't have a good time. when i'm finally at the end of the comic and look up at david, there's sticky marshmallow all over his face.

"you can ask them why they didn't talk to you when they come over later."

"they don't come over every day."

"but it's time they came over, isn't it, lila? it's been almost a week since you went to mike's."

my stomach starts to hurt. what if they never come back again? maybe they aren't supposed to be out at night and i got them in a whole bunch

of trouble. not many people are allowed out when
i am.

"maybe they went on vacation," i say. i think about
them being out in the desert like talia tears. i picture them dancing around a cactus in their tutus.

"maybe," david says.

"they could have colds and not be allowed out or
have some kind of chicken pox or something."

"chicken pox?"

"yeah, they could have itchy bumps all over and
not be able to leave the house."

david looks at me and picks marshmallow off his
face to eat like he's been saving it for a snack later.

"yeah, and maybe they got grabbed by aliens or
bigfoot or something on the way to your house . . ."

"i guess that could have happened too. but they
could just have homework and stuff and not be able
to come out, even though they never talk about
school to me."

"i've never seen them at school," david says.

"they probably go to private school."

david goes over to the front window and makes faces in it. it blocks all the sun from coming in. all of it. every day is a cloudy day in our house. cool. cloudy.

i can't wait for the sun.

"what if they don't ever come back and bring me the rest of the sun bag stuff?"

"they'll come back, lila."

"they're the only ones who know all the sun secrets. i can't do it without them. the bag won't have enough things in it."

"i'll help you, lila, if they don't come back."

"thanks."

"but i know they'll come."

"how do you know?" i say.

"i just do."

"tell me how you just do."

david starts taking all his magnificent mutant comic books out of his backpack. we always trade them with each other. he pushes the new one at me.

"this is the one where talia tears is put in the water

tank because she found out that some hackers were going to take all the water in the world for themselves. but the hackers are dumb 'cause they listened to luke when he begged them not to put her in water. he just knew they'd do the opposite and talia would get her strength back and save everybody."

"just like you know alyssa and elizabeth will be back."

david picks more marshmallow off his face, lies back down on the floor, and starts reading again.

"uh-huh. just like that."

and then i think of talia tears in the water tank building up her superpowers and saving the world. it might not seem like it, but i'm building up my powers too. maybe not to save the world, but i'll have saved them up for when i need them.

15

)

i remember that the first thing alyssa ever
said to me was about how her cat joey was mad at
everybody.

last year when i was sitting in the backyard looking at our moonflowers—she was there.

her wings were big that night, and her tutu was
moon-glow blue.

i thought she was a real fairy.

i wondered, should i ask for a wish?

she said, "hi, my cat joey is mad at me and my

sister, so we thought we'd come over here and meet you."

and then elizabeth was there, brushing herself off after climbing underneath the fence. leaves and ferns stuck to her.

she said, "did you tell her joey was mad at us, so we needed to come meet her?"

"yep."

"did you tell her we've been wanting to meet her for a long time, but since joey is mad, this was a better time than any other?"

"kinda."

they glowed in the light coming from our kitchen.

i said, "are you fairies?" but then i felt my face getting real warm and for a few seconds i was sorry i'd asked.

until elizabeth said, "maybe."

alyssa grabbed her hand and said it too. "maybe."

i remember i showed them all the things in my yard. i showed them how you could read in our big oak tree if you lie on your stomach just right with a flashlight. alyssa liked that, but kept falling out and laughing. it was only a little fall, she'd say.

i showed them where i was digging to antarctica to find penguins and glaciers. i showed them where i'd have a big clubhouse one day and where the moon-flowers bloom.

we ran around the yard all night.

we sang.

we told stories.

and just around the time i usually went in, after the clock in our kitchen rang four bells, alyssa and elizabeth grabbed hands again and walked over to the fence.

"bye, lila," they both said at the same time, then disappeared under the fence.

i was so happy i had night friends that i didn't even stop to remember that i'd never told alyssa and elizabeth my name and that they'd never told me theirs either. we all just knew.

*　★　*

they hadn't said they'd come back, but i wanted to be ready the next night in case they did.

monk had made us brownies and lemonade and her boyfriend mikal helped me ice the brownies with pictures of fairies.

"they'll like these," i said.

"who wouldn't?" mikal said.

"can i meet them?" monk asked. "they sound like fun, lila."

"uh-huh. just go to the backyard tonight. you'll meet them."

"cool," monk said. then she and mikal took off in his car for the city.

the rest of the day i read comics, played video games, and practiced french with mama, who made me learn stuff even in the summertime. i don't get vacation like the kids who go to the big brick school across from the park.

i waited for the sun to get low. i sat up in the tree, smelling the honeysuckle and listening to the crickets. then they were there.

alyssa had a pinwheel and elizabeth a handle bag
that said *maple grove mall*. there were watercolor paint-
ings of the ocean on one side. fish and star-fish.
there were drawings on the other side of the sun
shining on a beach full of people.

"here it is, lila," alyssa said.

i reached for the pinwheel, but they pushed the
bag at me.

"what is it?" i looked in, smiled.

"it's your sun bag," alyssa said.

elizabeth saw the brownies over on the picnic
bench and was there before alyssa could tell me the
rest. in a few minutes almost all the brownies were
gone and we were playing flashlight tag all over the
backyard.

that night, that second night, i really wanted wings
and tutus just like the girls. i wanted to fly off the
ground (or look like i could). i wanted to always
seem to be dancing even if i was just skipping across
the cool dark grass.

when the sun was almost up, alyssa and elizabeth

crawled back under the fence. i wished i could follow them. and when elizabeth came back under the
fence, i thought she was inviting me. but it was the
pinwheel she wanted.

then she whispered in my ear. she smelled like
the outdoors and pennies.

"when we fill the bag, you can play in the sun."

then she was gone.

monk told me she was sorry she'd missed alyssa and
elizabeth that night. she said she should have come
back before ten o'clock. i didn't understand how
she didn't see them then. they were in the backyard
until the sun was almost up.

i didn't want to hurt monk's feelings, though, so
i just said, "next time, monk. you'll meet them the
next time."

16

you can be a part of anything in the dark if you have night eyes, ears, and a nose.

i'm used to it and good at it. i'd like to stand outside in the daytime and see as well. i think people are more easy with themselves in the dark, though, 'cause they don't have to worry about people looking at them.

i can smell mr. selner's cigarette from five doors down when he stands outside smoking at two in the morning. his wife doesn't know he still smokes.

michelle palmer across the street always pushes her car into their driveway so her parents won't hear her come in after her curfew.

ms. kelling on the corner waters her yard even when it hasn't rained in a long time and the city people say you can't. she makes sure the sidewalk doesn't get wet.

mr. gallucci eats pizza and potato chips at night in his car even though the doctor tells him not to. he always hands me slices out the window and is the most happy man while he's eating.

i like my neighborhood when it's dark. the secrets in people come out. but i'd never tell on them. that would be cheating.

17

there are two things in the bag now, but i look at them all the time.

sometimes i just sit and look at the things in it.

sometimes i just hold the bag and think what it's going to be like when i run out on the beach with nothing but a swimsuit on. or run after the ice cream truck in the middle of the day after i've been in the sprinklers in the backyard.

but sometimes i wonder how it's all going to work. i wonder how the sun bag is going to fix everything.

i found something under the tree last night. a note on it said *from us*.

more for the bag. the girls are back.

it'll only take two more. alyssa and elizabeth said it will only take two more and i believe it. but i'm starting to get a little nervous. my stomach has been butterfly-nervous since i saw the girls at big mike's department store.

i think i might have made a mistake. maybe the girls in the store just looked like alyssa and elizabeth.

when i wake up, there's a bowl of fruit and a sandwich in foil next to my bed. monk must have brought it all 'cause it's mama and dad's night to go out. i'm sorry i missed them before they left.

i like to stand in the door and watch mama put her lipstick on. i like the way she puts it on me while i lean toward her and look in the mirror.

i have a round face. not like mama's. her face is skinny and long with turned-up lines around her mouth. mama calls them laugh lines. i like them. i can't wait till i have some of my own.

i crunch into an apple and think how it's going to be when i can get some of those lines and go out in the sun without hats and glasses and layers of clothes.

i'm almost finished eating the fruit in the bowl when my bedroom window goes up and alyssa crawls in.

there's mud up to her knees and her face is wet.

"it's raining out there, lila."

i make a place for her on the bed.

"oh, yeah. i didn't even hear it."

"yep, there's big puddles."

she looks at the bowl and i pass it over to her. she eats the few grapes and the banana that are left in it.

sometimes i put cookies and peanut butter sandwiches in bags around the yard for her and elizabeth. the food always disappears by the next day.

mama says my appetite's getting just as good as alyssa's and elizabeth's.

who cares about appetites. i leave them food 'cause they're my friends.

like david.

like monk, even though she is my sister.

"you wanna go out and play in the puddles?" alyssa says.

i do.

a few minutes later we're splashing around the backyard.

alyssa's wings start to droop from being too wet.

my tennis shoes are brown and squishy from all the water, but we keep running and splashing. and i don't even think to ask alyssa where elizabeth is until we are crawling around in the clubhouse.

when i do, alyssa puts her thumb in her mouth.

then she points.

i can't really tell where she's pointing 'cause we're in the clubhouse and it's dark. i figure maybe she wants me to guess.

so i say, "is she in the tree?"

alyssa grins. "no."

"is she on the roof?"

"no."

"is she on top of the fence?"

alyssa giggles. "no."

after i ask if she's in our tub or david's garage (she could have been, 'cause i was stuck in there before), alyssa just shakes her head.

i figure it's none of my business to ask anymore, so we just sit and listen to the crickets. i can hear monk moving around in the kitchen and i think maybe i should go in and finally let her meet alyssa. but it seems like only a few minutes later that monk's waking me up, saying it's time to come in.

i'm in the kitchen doing my multiplication when i look out the window and see elizabeth. she goes into the clubhouse and brings out a pair of wings. alyssa must have left them last night.

i run over to the door and holler out to her, "where were you?"

but elizabeth only smiles and waves to me. then

as she's about to go back under the fence she yells, "guess."

   i can't guess so i go back to doing my numbers.

   mama says, "what's up?"

   i can't think of anything too good so i just say, "guess."

it'll be just like a movie, me walking on the beach in the sun. seagulls will fly over and dive-bomb fish out in the water. there'll be so many umbrellas in so many colors, but i won't get underneath any. i won't mind the sun. it's going to be warm on my face with no blisters or burning.

   there won't be any scars or worse later either. 'cause it'll be okay now. it'll be just okay, the way monk says things are when something that's been hard is finally over. or the way mama says it's okay after i spill something on the floor.

   i'll be able to walk to school with all the neighborhood kids, and me and david will go to the drugstore for comic books.

we'll sit out in the field by the park and read
magnificent mutants until the sun starts to go
down. i'll have to go home then 'cause most people
have to be in by the time it gets dark.

i'll be like most people.

AND EVERYTHING ELSE

18

minnie bell hiccups when we slow down at
the red light. the whole inside of the car glows red.
david sneezes in the backseat.

"bless you," i say, and wave my arm out the window 'cause monk lets me do it and mama and dad
don't.

just as we go by the azalea house, the lights flash
on. i can almost hear the hum. david and me start
to laugh.

monk says, "what?"

david sneezes again.

"you allergic to something?" monk asks as she pulls minnie bell onto the highway.

david says, "nope."

"you catchin' a cold then?"

"nope," david says, and then sneezes again.

monk starts laughing and turns the music up real loud.

we all like the song that's on the radio a whole lot, so we sing it as loud as we can. david sings loudest even though he sneezes through most of it.

david and me drink so many milk shakes at fallen angel we can barely move away from the booth by the window. i'm so happy he's here. his mom almost didn't let him come, but his dad just waved him out of the house, saying, "let the kid go."

"i don't get to come into the city much," david says. "i like it."

"i like it too," david says as he watches two people move a bed down the street. "i could live here."

"yeah, the city is always awake. if i lived here there would always be people up. it wouldn't be just me and elizabeth and alyssa."

"but they only come to your house sometimes."

"yep, they do come only sometimes. but always when i'm missing them."

david slurps his banana shake till it's all gone. i spoon chocolate chips into my strawberry-banana shake and laugh at him.

i guess we're laughing real loud 'cause monk and her friends look over at us and smile.

the waitress with the dragonfly tattoo comes over and smiles at us too.

"having a good time?"

"yeah," i say.

david keeps slurping.

"i like your hat," she says to me.

"thanks. i always wear them 'cause i'm not friends with the sun, even when it's dark out."

the waitress nods and then goes over to a table where everybody knows her. they call her callie and all of them order coffee.

it's only when i look back out the window that i see them. but by the time i grab david's arm to point at them, they're gone.

i keep pointing out the window.

"it's them, david. they followed us to the city. how'd they get here? did they take a bus? the train?"

"who?"

david twists around in his seat and stares real hard out the window. taxis fly by. horns blow and people are just getting out of a movie across the street.

i get up and run to the door. so does david.

"it's them."

"it's who, lila?"

"it's alyssa and elizabeth."

"where?" david almost yells.

monk is looking at us like she's about to come over and make us sit with her and her friends. and we don't want to do that, so we both go back to our booth and just look at each other.

"did you really see them, lila?"

i did, but david looks like he doesn't believe me.

"why would they be here?"

i let the chocolate melt on my tongue and feel tired.

and then i start to know what i really don't want to know.

david doesn't understand how important alyssa and elizabeth are to me. and i don't know how to tell him.

"too bad you missed 'em," he says.

"yeah," i say, and keep watching, 'cause in the city two girls in fairy wings and tutus standing on the sidewalk wouldn't even make people look.

it's raining when monk tells us to put our seat belts on. david yawns. monk turns on the music, but real low this time. the rain is soft and makes me sleepy. i know i'll be asleep before we go over the bridge.

but it's then that i see them.

they're running behind the car.

somebody must have left them here, in the rain.

they're holding each other's hands as they run.

i scream for monk to stop the car.

"somebody must have left them, monk. we've got to go back for them."

monk pulls the car over, almost onto the sidewalk.

"who got left, lila? where?"

monk has a scared look on her face when she turns around and looks at me. david is wide awake now, and even in the dark i know he's looking at me. he knows who i mean.

he leans over the front seat and puts his hand on monk's shoulder before she opens the door. buses and cars are speeding by so fast, i'm worried she'll be hurt when she goes to get the girls.

"it's alyssa and elizabeth," david says. "she thinks she sees alyssa and elizabeth."

his voice is so soft, it's a whisper.

monk starts the car up again, then pulls minnie bell out into traffic.

i'm about to start yelling at monk to stop, but when i look back, they're gone, and there are so many cars and buses that i start to wonder how they could have been running to us in the street anyway.

monk is asleep beside me when i wake up in the morning. her arms are wrapped around me in the shadows that the covers make. she is snoring, real soft.

it makes me smile. then it reminds me of david whispering.

she *thinks* she sees alyssa and elizabeth.

19

the house that hums is all lighted up now.
i stand in front of it and pull some of the azalea
leaves off the bushes.

everybody says that nobody lives there.

david and me have watched the house a thousand
times. we watch the lights go on. we watch the shadows
from all the bushes dance all across the lighted-up
windows.

i don't think the house is haunted or anything.
just lonely. i understand that sometimes. sometimes.

david went to his grandparents' in michigan, and monk and mikal went to visit friends for the weekend. so i'm just standing here listening to the house hum and missing everybody.

dad calls me from his car. he's on his way to work.

"what you up to, kid?"

i go over to the car and lean into the open window.

"not doing anything, dad."

he's sipping coffee out of his green car mug and listening to the radio. sometimes he listens to the same music me and monk do.

"i hope you're not going to trespass into the neighbors' yard."

"what's trespass?"

dad takes another sip of coffee and turns down the music. "trespass is going onto someone's property without being asked."

"oh."

"so you aren't going to, right?"

"right."

"good." then dad reaches over and squeezes my face. i watch his car until he turns the corner. then i'm right back in front of the humming house.

i miss everybody.

haven't seen alyssa and elizabeth since we went to the city about two weeks ago. i'm worried that they never got home from there. what if they're still wandering around in the streets?

i worried that night, but monk told me it was okay. she said they'd be back and that i had probably just seen two kids who looked like them.

i didn't believe her, but it was too late to go get them after we were out of the city. they haven't been back since then, and david's gone for a while.

i walk back home and crawl into my clubhouse. mama is talking to someone on the phone, laughing and making plans for the next day. her voice puts me to sleep.

it's not a dream when i wake up and find alyssa and elizabeth running around the yard. i'm so happy to see them that i run out of the clubhouse and scream, "you're here!"

both of them are dressed exactly alike tonight. all in white. elizabeth's wings are so big i'm afraid a big wind might make her fly away. alyssa runs over to me and laughs.

"i was worried," i say.

"worried about what?" they say together.

"worried that i'd never see you both again."

they turn and look at each other.

"we're always here, lila."

then they grab my hand.

"is anybody home?" they say, pointing at the house.

"my mama's home."

"that's good," alyssa says.

it's like always. we run all over the yard and play into the night. elizabeth reads us a book about trolls and castles, which i'm too old to believe in, but she likes them so much i let her read on.

*   *   *

there's pink in the sky when i wake up in my sleeping bag under the tree. a few fireflies are still sparkling around the yard. they remind me of alyssa and elizabeth.

i look over at the fence, expecting to see them just leaving. but they're not there. i go over to look underneath. i can never find that part of the fence after elizabeth and alyssa leave. i've tried again and again, but now's my chance.

the sky is turning pinker when i get to the broken board in the fence. mama calls me and i turn around to look at the house. when i turn back to the fence, the broken board is gone.

just like that.

i pick up one more thing for the sun bag.

20

i watch a video of mama pushing me in a baby stroller. monk is trying to pull dad off into an arcade with someone dressed up like a lion in front of it.

he goes inside with her.

mama smiles and waves at whoever is taking the video. she bends down and grabs hold of one of my fat baby legs and shakes it at the camera. then she takes off my booties and waves my feet at it too.

i don't know where we were, but it's night there.

and everybody is smiling and i'm not covered

up and my stroller isn't draped in sun-blocking blankets.

i only remember night vacations.

niagara falls is beautiful at night. the ocean is loud and scary. the mountains could be huge monsters just waiting for you. i'm used to taking my vacations in the dark.

i get to go out in the daytime only for emergencies. and i don't think i'd like to be covered up totally. i like the nighttime vacations.

now is the part of the tape where monk is feeding me ice cream at an outside restaurant. i eat all the ice cream and cry for more. for the first time i notice that monk is probably the same age in the video that i am now. and she looks just like me except she's in a sundress and sandals.

the video ends.

21

david brought me so many old copies of the mutants from his grandma's house that i've been sitting around all day just reading. mama has yelled at me five times to get up and do my chores.

i go and do them, but she says i'm not doing them well. i got all the stuff off of my bedroom floor, even though i did put it underneath the bed. i straightened up the bathroom and she didn't tell me not to put dirty clothes and wet towels into the tub.

it's a day of yelling for mama, but i've got talia tears to keep me happy so i don't mind so much.

david comes over a little later, and we both go out back under the stars with flashlights to read more magnificent mutants. his mom is out with friends now and his brother doesn't care.

"i didn't know the mutants had been around so long," david says as he's starting to read from my pile. "these were my dad's and he has to be in his thirties, so they're real old."

"your grandma saved his comics?"

"no, she didn't save 'em. he hid them in the rafters in their garage so she wouldn't throw them away."

"wow," i say, and run my hand over the page where talia tears has just made a big wave and washed out all the bad guys in the woods.

"it's funny thinking of your dad reading comics."

"he read them the whole time we were at grandma's. me and him just sat out in the backyard reading all day long. pretty cool for my dad. grandma had to yell at us to come in to dinner and go on the family picnic. we could have read the mutants forever."

"me too," i say, thinking about how mama has been giving me dirty looks all day. but it doesn't matter 'cause david is back and talia tears has to fly a plane over a volcano 'cause even though the pilot is mutating into the winged warrior and the only thing he can do is fly (on his own wings) and use a sword, he's evil and no help to talia.

if i were ever a superhero, i'd call myself the sun goddess/moon girl.

moon girl would wear a dress made of white owl feathers held together with spiderwebs. she would be able to see in the dark and fly up tall buildings.

sun goddess would be able to make fire whenever she wanted to and could disappear and reappear anywhere. she could go into volcanoes and even up to the sun itself.

i like the idea that she'd have two people in her and never have to wait for day or night to have power. but it's not so bad to have just one power, i guess. i see in the dark better than most people and hear things at night hardly anybody else does.

i want to be a sort of superhero. maybe i am already, just a little.

22

monk is decorating the yard for my birthday party.

    she dances around and throws ribbons over trees
and even the big willow branches that peek into our
yard from the neighbors' house. now the branches
are swinging red and white ribbons for my party.

    i dance around and throw ribbons too, but the
ribbons don't fall all nice like monk's do. i need to
be taller.

    mama is watching us and laughing.

"i hope we have good weather for the party," i say.

monk throws blue ribbons at me and laughs. "we're supposed to."

"been weather-watching again?" mama says. she picks up a shiny gold star and ties it to the big tree.

"can't hurt to keep checking the forecast," monk says. "it won't rain on lila's birthday party."

"yeah," i say, and throw more ribbon.

i want to tell monk and mama that they didn't have to plan my party for nighttime. it would be just fine in the day. but i can't. it might be too hard for them to believe that my bag holds all the secrets to the daylight.

i leave the backyard, and it's so pretty that i back out of the gate so i can keep looking at it. there are twinkly lights, moons, stars, suns, and everything else hanging from the big tree and even the house.

it's beautiful.

i still have one more sun thing to get.

just one more.

*   *   *

alyssa and elizabeth haven't been around much since david got back from his grandma's and i've been a little busy—what with reading all the magnificent mutant comics, planning my party, and thinking about how everything will change in a couple of days.

and last night i met a girl named jackie who came into the yard to read comic books with me. she said she'd just moved in a street away.

she was nice, even though she liked galaxia gorgon better than talia tears. and she didn't even eat all the brownies dad set out on the table.

i started to tell her about how alyssa and elizabeth always ate every last one, but i decided not to. i don't know why, but i didn't tell. i did invite her to my party, though.

maybe another time i'll tell her about them.

i went to bed early last night, sleepier than usual. i didn't even think about the girls showing up.

23

it's night now. my party starts in a little while and david, jackie, and me are standing in front of the humming house. it looks even scarier than it usually does.

jackie wants to go look in the windows.

i say that we shouldn't 'cause my dad told me about what trespass means.

david never has gone in the yard and looked in the windows, but he's always wanted to.

jackie's dad probably never told her what trespass

means and she just likes it that the house makes a humming noise.

she's wearing black tennis shoes and a yellow t-shirt over striped yellow-and-black shorts. david has been teasing her and buzzing around her, calling her bumble. she laughs, showing her tonsils, and pulls on her braids while she's trying to get us to look in the window of the humming house.

"my dad says the humming sound is just the air conditioner in the house," david says.

"oh yeah?" jackie says.

david looks at me like there's nothing we should be afraid of then.

"come on," jackie says, then raises an azalea branch and heads up the front walk. you can hardly see the walk for all the bushes.

jackie is a round light of yellow.

we follow her and i get goose bumps up my arms just from walking under the azaleas. i can hear david behind me laughing like he does when he's doing something he's not supposed to do.

even though i'm scared, i think this is one of the best things i've ever done, trespassing onto the humming house.

jackie has beat me and david to the living room window. her face is pressed to the glass before we get there. but suddenly the house hums loud and all the lights come on.

jackie screams. she's new and didn't expect the light.

david laughs again.

i stand under the azaleas until jackie says, "oooohhh."

then my feet move me closer to her and the window. i can feel david behind me. wings. i remember the wings.

david whispers, "what is it?"

"wings," i say.

jackie's face is still pressed to the window, her head moving from side to side. i don't think she hears us. she looks like she's dreaming.

when she turns to us, she has a big smile on her

face. david and me grab hands and walk up to the window of the trespass house. then i hear the music and remember the song.

we listen to the piano song like ballerinas dance to. and with all three of our faces pressed against the glass we watch as two little ballerinas dance. one in pink, the other in white, both in big sparkling wings.

they dance together like they always have. they whirl and twirl at the same time and are so perfect together, even though one wears rain boots.

but when the music stops, the dancers stop and the hum is just a hum again as both of them stand still on top of the music box in front of the window.

we keep listening for the hum and the music. but then i feel something underneath my tennis shoes. two somethings. they're the last piece for my sun bag. i pick them up and hold them in back of me. i stand close to my friends, though.

close to all of them.

24

my sun pieces circle around my bed. i've spaced them out, taken out each thing and held it in my hand awhile.

there's a real old spinning top with bears and tigers on it. the bears look like they're dancing. one might be the bear alyssa had to fight. it glows in the dark, like . . .

maybe a stingray in a fishbowl.

or a bowl full of fireflies, maybe.

the tigers are jumping through hoops of fire. i

think of spinning with fireflies all over me.

there's a book with pictures of people with animal heads. it's brown and old-smelling, with shiny gold lines around the pages. i like it. i look through the pages and think of the magnificent mutants.

the third thing is dragonfly stickers. some glow. all have different colors, and i think how the waitress at the fallen angel beanery would have a hard time choosing which one she'd like to have tattooed on her other ankle.

so much light is coming from the fourth thing that i think it might be the sun itself. but it's a locket that glitters. i hold it and think awhile.

the last thing—the thing from the humming house—is feathers. two golden feathers that are so small, so soft that they have to be from fairy wings. they have to be.

and i'm wondering how i thought i'd be able to stand in the sun when all these things were together.

25

it's getting darker now.

i'm sitting on my bedroom floor in my birthday dress. i hear the back gate opening and closing. i hear david, and monk starts laughing at something somebody says.

i'm still waiting.

now the twinkly lights are on in the backyard and the sky is more gray than pink. the sun is gone and more people have come. i invited the neighborhood and never thought that adults might not come because they'd think it was just a nine-year-old's party. they all came.

there are mushrooms that glow in the dark. i still don't remember when i found out about them, and since i never asked alyssa and elizabeth, i guess i'll have to figure it out myself.

i hear dad calling my name. i hear the music and people laughing. i can smell vanilla, and i know monk baked what i love best to eat.

    mikal is dancing with jackie, and david is staring at mr. rocko, who monk borrowed for the night and brought to my party. he's wearing a tuxedo jacket.

    i run out of my room and down the stairs, smelling vanilla and ready for my party. but something stops me at the kitchen doors.

    the night in the backyard is lit up. everybody is surrounded by blinking lights.

    fireflies.

    hundreds of them.

i walk out into the middle of the yard and wander through the blinking lights, fireflies all around.

i put my arms way out at my sides and the fireflies start to land on me. david stands near me and whispers, "why are they doing that?"

i don't say anything. i just let them sit on my arms. they aren't tickly 'cause i've got long sleeves on. they just sit and blink.

in a while, though, i feel them tickling my head. then my neck.

everybody stands there with their mouths wide open. the party stops. but that's okay, 'cause it's my party. i'm the moon girl with fireflies. i'm all lit up.

i close my eyes. i think this feels better than the sun ever could. i start to twirl, but just a little. the fireflies don't leave, and i know that they want to be with me.

superhero me.

moon girl, firefly keeper, superhero me.

when i open my eyes, everybody is still standing where they were.

ms. kelling takes a picture. david's brother looks

like he's expecting more fireflies to land on everybody.

monk and mikal hold hands and shake their heads with big smiles on their faces.

mrs. gallucci and mr. palmer from across the street whisper that they should call the city to report all the fireflies. jackie is laughing.

mama stands behind monk and mikal. she's crying. then she's laughing at the same time. just crying and laughing like she's trying each one out. dad winks at me and looks up.

but i just keep twirling real slow so i won't get dizzy and the fireflies will hang around me for a while.

i want to keep my birthday fireflies as long as i can. i want to keep my blinking, flying birthday lights all over me.

26

i've always wanted to be nine. always wanted to be nine and a superhero. always wanted to be
nine, a superhero, and able to go out in the sun in
a swimsuit on a bright hot day.

now i am nine.

i might be a superhero.

but being out in the sun doesn't really matter
anymore 'cause *it's* there and *i'm* here. that's just how
it is.

i don't see alyssa and elizabeth like i did before. i

do see them, but not in the backyard. i see them in dreams and when i'm thinking about before. i don't think about how i used to see them. it's not important to talk about it all anymore, or tell any-one who doesn't already know.

the telling is over. talia tears would just wash it all away. so i think i'll do like her. just wash it all away.

i don't have to be the sun goddess. i'm really okay being a moon girl.

there's nothing wrong with moon girls.